RUDE ROWDY RUMORS

A Brian and Pea Brain Mystery

RUDE ROWDY RUMORS

by **ELIZABETH LEVY**

illustrated by **George Ulrich**

■ HarperCollins*Publishers*

c · 1

*To Sandra Pereira
and everybody at Molly Fox*

Library of Congress Cataloging-in-Publication Data
Levy, Elizabeth
    Rude rowdy rumors : a Brian and Pea Brain mystery / by Elizabeth
Levy ; illustrated by George Ulrich.
        p.   cm.
    Summary: Seven-year-old Brian enlists the help of his little sister
Penny to discover which of his soccer teammates is spreading rumors
about him.
    ISBN 0-06-023462-8. — ISBN 0-06-023463-6 (lib. bdg.)
    [1. Soccer—Fiction.   2. Brothers and sisters—Fiction.   3. Mystery
and detective stories.]   I. Ulrich, George, ill.   II. Title.
PZ7.L5827Rp   1994   93-46792
[Fic]—dc20   CIP
                                                                  AC

1 2 3 4 5 6 7 8 9 10
❖
First Edition

Contents

Sock It to Me

"Are you going to play real baseball again this year?" Penny Casanova asked her brother Brian. She used her thumbs to push the buttons on her electronic baseball game. She giggled. Penny had just inherited the game from Brian while he was cleaning out his room. Brian had said that he didn't want it anymore. But hearing the buzzes and beeps again made him want to play.

"Give me a turn," Brian begged.

"No," said Penny. "It's mine. You said it was a stupid game."

"Come on, I just want to play one game," said Brian.

Penny shook her head gleefully. "If you're going to play real baseball, you should be practicing. Shouldn't he practice, Mookie?" Penny asked.

Mookie was Brian's best friend. He had come over to help Brian clean up his room, but now they both wanted to play with the electronic game that Brian felt he had stupidly given to his little sister.

Brian glared at Penny. He stunk at baseball and his little sister Penny knew it. He was dreading the spring. It was bad enough that spring meant flowers and hay fever and asthma attacks. Spring also meant baseball. Baseball was worse than asthma. Brian took a whiff from his inhaler that helped clear his lungs. The very thought of baseball was enough to give him an asthma attack.

Brian tried to use his brain to tell his

hands where to go to catch the ball, but his hands just never got to the right place. When he was up at bat, the most Brian could hope for was a walk. Brian hated to admit it, but he wished the whole world of sports would just go away.

"You know, we don't have to play baseball," said Mookie.

"Yeah," said Penny. "You could sit around on your rear ends all the time. Brian is a couch potato! Brian is a coach potato!" Penny jumped up and down on the couch. Penny always had a lot of energy.

"We don't have to be couch potatoes either," said Mookie. "The peewee soccer league is going to have a spring minicamp this year. I picked up a flyer about it on the way over here. I'm going to play. Why don't you join too?"

Brian shrugged. "I don't know. It doesn't seem like much fun."

"Soccer's great," said Mookie. "Have you ever tried it?"

Brian shook his head. He hadn't played because he was worried that he would stink at soccer just as he did at baseball. He didn't want to fail at yet another sport.

"Brian doesn't like to do things he's not good at," said Penny.

Brian made a face. "I'd like to sock her," he said to Mookie. "Can I do that?"

"Ma!" screamed Penny. "Brian's going to sock it to me."

"I am not," hissed Brian, snapping his hand around Penny's mouth. Brian was always getting in trouble for being mean to Penny. He didn't think it was fair. Penny was plenty mean to him, but because he was older he always got in trouble.

"Come on, you two," said Mookie.

Mookie sometimes got tired of their fighting. "Let's go outside. I'll get my ball and we can practice dribbling."

"Oh, good. I'll watch," said Penny. "I love to watch Brian dribble. When he's drinking milk and he laughs, he's real good at dribbling."

"See what I have to put up with?" said Brian. "You're lucky your sisters are older."

"Yeah right," said Mookie. "They pick on me anyway."

Just as they were leaving the house the phone rang. Mrs. Casanova picked it up. She waved to them. "It's Uncle Mike," she said. "Come say hello."

Penny ran to the phone. She loved her Uncle Mike and Aunt Sarah who lived in California. "Uncle Mike, guess what," shouted Penny. She always shouted on the phone when it was long distance.

"Brian's going to play soccer. He's a dribbler. You know that yucky thing he does with his milk. I'm going to be a great soccer player too."

Brian made a face. He hated it when Penny told news about him. He grabbed the phone.

"It's not such a big deal," he told his uncle.

"It's a very interesting game," said Uncle Mike. "But then you know what the sock said to the foot."

"No," said Brian, but he knew a bad joke was coming.

"You're putting me on," said Uncle Mike. He gave a belly laugh that could be heard by all the Casanovas and Mookie. "Well we're coming to visit in a couple of weeks," continued Uncle Mike. "Maybe I'll get to see you play."

"Great," said Brian. He handed the

phone to his dad.

"We'll be careful to lock away the good china," teased Mr. Casanova when he got on the phone.

Mrs. Casanova's brother was famous for two things, his bad jokes and the fact that he had two left feet. All he had to do was to walk into a room and something would break.

After he hung up, Brian's dad looked at Brian. "Are you really going to play soccer?" he asked.

"Me too," said Penny. "It sounds like fun."

"You're too little," said Brian, pointing to the flyer. "See here. It says kids seven and older. You're only five. You're just in kindergarten. I am seven. I'm old enough"

Penny looked at the brochure. "It says seven to ten years old," she read proudly.

She had just learned to pick out numbers when they were written out. "Brian, you're going to be the youngest, probably the shortest, and definitely the dribbliest kid there."

"Penny," warned their father. "That's not nice. Brian might be very good at soccer."

Mrs. Casanova gave Brian a funny look.

"What?" Brian asked his mother.

"Nothing," said Mrs. Casanova thoughtfully. "I just always thought you took after Uncle Mike. He's so good with his brain."

Uncle Mike taught science. Brian gave his mother a dirty look. He knew that his mother thought that he also took after Uncle Mike in being the world's biggest klutz.

Zap and the Grouch

Just two days later, Brian's mother handed Brian an Express Mail package from California.

"Nothing for me?" asked Penny. She watched as Brian ripped open the package. He pulled out a big book called *All About Soccer* by Jared Lebow.

"Neat," said Brian, reading the note attached to the book. "Uncle Mike says that this was written by a friend of his. He says that I can learn lots of secrets about soccer from this book. He also asks what did the big toe say to the little toe?"

"I don't know," said Penny. She couldn't believe Uncle Mike hadn't send her a present.

"There's a big heel following us."

Brian started leafing through the book. Penny was bored.

When Mookie came over Brian showed him the book. "You can't learn soccer from a book," said Mookie.

Brian made a face. He *liked* learning from books.

"He's Brian Brain, not Brian Star Athlete," said Penny. When Penny was little she couldn't say Brian, so she'd call him Brain. Then Brian started calling her Pea Brain because she was so little, and the names stuck.

"I'm a student of the game," said Brian. The truth was that all the diagrams in the book about soccer seemed complicated, and he couldn't make head nor tail out of them.

"If you're a student of the game, then you've gotta play," said Mookie. "There's nothing like real-life experience."

"Brian doesn't like real life," said Penny.

Brian glared at her. "Okay, I'll go," he said.

"Great," said Mookie. "Come on. Some of the kids are getting together in the park. I'll introduce you. And you can fill out an application."

Brian followed Mookie across the park. Penny trailed along too. There was a group of kids playing a pickup game of soccer. One particularly big kid got the ball away from a girl trying to get around him. Then the girl pushed him hard, got the ball back, and got around him.

"Hey!" shouted the boy.

"That's Oscar Potler," whispered Mookie. "He's in the second grade too. He's the sweeper. The coach says that he's got what it takes to be a star. But he hasn't reached his potential."

"What's a sweeper?" asked Brian. He hadn't gotten to that in his book.

"That's the guy who will kill you if you get past him. He's in the last line of defense between the goalie and the attacker. Natalia's the attacker."

"Attacker?" said Penny, who was listening. "Are you gonna be attacked?"

"No, if anybody's going to be the attacker, it's going to be me," bragged Brian, not feeling at all sure of himself.

The kids took a break. "Good going, Natalia," said Mookie. "Hey, guys, I want you to meet a friend of mine. He's going to come to the minicamp. Maybe with him, we'll finally win a game."

"You mean your team doesn't win?" asked Penny, sounding shocked.

Mookie shrugged. "We lost all our games last fall," he admitted. "That's why we're having this minicamp."

Brian felt his stomach relax. If the team had never won, then he probably couldn't hurt their chances much.

Natalia punched Brian on the arm. It hurt. Brian didn't have very strong muscles in his arms.

"What do you call yourself?" Natalia asked.

"Brian Casanova," said Brian.

"Naw. We all have nicknames. Like mine is Zap, because I zap defenders. We call Mookie Mook the Nuke. That big tub of lard I got the ball around is the Grouch."

"My name is really Oscar," he admitted. "I like being called the Grouch

because I'm a fierce defender."

"Yeah, a defender of nothing," teased Natalia. "You're so easy to get around. Anyhow all great soccer players have nicknames. You should think of one for yourself."

"I've got one," said Penny. "Strike Out."

"They don't have strikeouts in soccer, Pea Brain," said Brian. "I wish lightning would strike you."

"Lightning is a good name," interrupted Mookie. He didn't want his teammates to have to watch a fight between Pea Brain and Brian Brain.

Brian tried the word out in his head. "Lightning." He liked it.

"Lightning Brian Brain sounds like something from a science project," said Penny.

"Who's she?" asked Natalia.

16

"No one," said Brian. "Just my little sister."

Brian turned to Mookie. "Give me that application. I'm taking it home and filling it out right now."

"We'll see you, Lightning," said Natalia. "Our first practice is tomorrow."

As they walked back across the park. Brian bounded ahead. Penny gave Mookie a worried look. "Do you think he'll make the team?" she asked him.

Mookie shrugged. "Sure," he said. "All he's got to do is fill out the application. and he said he was going to do it right away."

Penny knew that Brain would have no trouble filling out the application. It was the soccer part that worried her. She knew Brian and sports.

3

Lightning Meets Flash

The next day as they walked to the practice field, Penny said quietly to Brian, "I really hope you make the team."

"Thanks," said Brian. He knew that Penny meant it. She wasn't all bad.

When they got to the practice field, Brian took one look at the other players and wished that the ground would swallow him.

There were a lot of kids, over two dozen of them, and they were all bigger than him—even the girls—especially the girls.

Penny's eyes got big. "You're gonna get cremated," she whispered. Two girls from Brian's class, Heather and her friend, Leticia, giggled when they saw Brian. Natalia whispered something to Oscar.

Coach Sandra Pereira blew her whistle. Coach Pereira was from Brazil. She was such a great star that people called her the female Pelé, after the greatest soccer player of all time who was also from Brazil. She had won a full scholarship to the university in their town to play soccer in the United States. When she had time she liked to teach soccer to kids.

"Good afternoon," said Coach Pereira. She spoke English with a slight lilting accent. "Everybody sit close so that you can all hear me. I recognize most of you. But I see a few new faces here. That's good. I have high hopes that finally we will get a group that pulls together.

Before, there was too much competition within our team. This is not a sport for stars. I want teamwork and hard work."

Coach Pereira had a soft voice. Penny inched closer. She wanted to hear what Coach Pereira was saying.

"The greatest stars are unselfish," continued Coach Pereira. "They want to raise everyone to their level. They don't want the glory for themselves."

Leticia raised her hand.

"You are a star," she said. "You get lots of glory."

"Only because I put the demands of my team first," said Coach Pereira. "As I said, today we have some newcomers. That pleases me. Would you stand up and introduce yourselves?"

Brian stood up. "Uh, my name's Brian Casanova," he muttered.

"Lightning Brian Casanova," shouted Penny.

Brian blushed.

Oscar nudged the girl standing next to him. "This is my cousin, Shauntrece," said Oscar, speaking for her. "She's a striker."

"So, you've played soccer before, Shauntrece," said Coach Pereira. Shauntrece nodded.

"They called me Flash on my other team," Shauntrece said. She smiled at Brian, but Brian wasn't sure it was a very friendly smile.

"How about you, Brian?" asked Coach Pereira.

"My nickname's Lightning," said Brian.

"No, I meant have you played much soccer?"

"Uh, I haven't really played, but I've read about it," said Brian.

A couple of the kids, especially Oscar, snickered.

"Read about it," giggled Shauntrece. "I haven't read any books about soccer."

"You don't need too," said Oscar. "You and me, we've got the feet for soccer. We've got soccer in our genes."

Penny looked at him. Oscar was a stocky kid. "You're jeans *are* a little tight," she said. "Besides, my brother is learning the secrets of soccer from my uncle."

Coach Pereira turned to Penny. "Are you here to play soccer too?" she asked.

"Yes," said Penny eagerly, bobbing her head up and down. Maybe they were going to change the rules for her.

"She is not," sputtered Brian. "She's my sister. She's only five. Can't you see? She's a shrimp."

Coach Pereira smiled at Penny warmly. "Some of the best soccer players are short. Look at me." Penny looked.

Coach Pereira did have short legs, but they were as sturdy as the trunk of a spruce tree. She looked rooted to the ground, and she carried her body high, with her stomach flat. Her arms were rounded with muscles. She looked strong. Penny wanted to grow up to look just like her.

"I'm only in kindergarten," confessed Penny.

Coach Pereira shook her head. "I'm sorry, that is too young for our team."

Brian sighed a breath of relief.

"I just want to watch so when I'm ready to play I'll know how to play unselfishly," said Penny.

Brian rolled his eyes. He couldn't imagine Penny playing unselfishly.

"That's good. I like to encourage players when they're young," said Coach Pereira.

"I'll do anything to help," Penny blurted out.

Brian groaned. He couldn't believe that Penny was hogging the attention on his first day of soccer practice. He hadn't even touched a ball yet, and she was the center of attention.

"Well, we can always use someone to help with the equipment and gather up the balls," said Coach Pereira.

"Great!" said Penny. She grinned.

Brian wasn't grinning.

The
Daily Moos

"You know," Penny explained to her parents, "I am a very important part of Brian's soccer team." She had been going to practice with Brian every day for over a week. "I'm the very official ball picker-upper."

Brian's nose was in the book that Uncle Mike had send him.

"Brian still thinks he can read about it instead of doing it," said Penny. "I love Coach Pereira. She's the coolest coach in the world."

"She's my coach, not yours," snapped Brian. He had to admit he kind of liked soccer. To his astonishment, he was actually pretty good at it — especially as a defender. Brian didn't like anybody messing with his turf.

The next day it rained all morning, and Brian thought they probably would not have practice. But soccer wasn't like baseball. You played soccer whether it rained or not. Penny put on her slicker.

After putting the team through their warm-up drills, Coach Pereira blew her whistle. "I'd like to get all our juices going with a few one-on-ones. Don't worry. It's just for fun, but this will give you a chance to get your feet wet." Coach Pereira laughed at her little joke.

Then she got serious. "Brian, I've been very impressed with your hard work and dedication. I think some of the rest of you could benefit from some of the study that Brian's been putting in. He's shaping up into one of the best defenders on our team. I'm proud of him."

Brian couldn't believe it. A coach was actually complimenting him. He beamed. He was determined not to let Coach Pereira down.

"Shauntrece, since you're also new, why don't you go up against Brian."

"Wait a minute," said Oscar. "I'm the team's best defender. You said last fall that I was the best young player you had ever seen. I'm the only young kid who's a starter. Shauntrece is too good for Brian. I should go against her."

"No, I want to see what Brian can do," said Coach Pereira firmly. "Penny, we don't have a goalie for these drills since I want it to be a true one-on-one, but just stand in the goal post and gather the ball back."

"Great! I can pretend to be the goalie. I want to be a goalie when I play."

Oscar growled. "You're just a ball picker-upper."

"Don't be such a grouch," said Penny.

"That's right, Oscar" said Coach Pereira easily. "You'll get plenty of chances later."

Shauntrece held her hand out to Brian. "Good luck," she said. Brian shook her hand. Her hand was much bigger than his.

Coach Pereira kicked the ball straight and true to Shauntrece. Then Shauntrece dribbled toward Brian, controlling the ball with her instep. Within a split second, she got in front of Brian and now there was nothing between her and the goal.

Brian felt humiliated. He huffed and puffed to catch up. Somehow he *had* to keep Shauntrece from kicking the ball into Penny's goal.

"Hey, Shauntrece," shouted Brian. His breath was ragged.

"Did you know that ancient Greeks blew up a cow's bladder to make the first soccer ball?" Brian hardly had enough breath to get out that long sentence, but he gasped it out.

Shauntrece took her eye off the ball for just a moment. "That's yucky. Why are you telling me this?"

"Because I hope it will slow you down," gasped Brian.

He had slowed her down. He got in front of her, standing between her and the goal. But Shauntrece still controlled the ball.

Penny stood ready. She liked pretending that she was the goalie, even if the job was just to pick up the ball. She had heard Brian's pathetic try to slow Shauntrece down.

"Hey, Shauntrece," yelled Penny. "What newspaper does a cow read?"

"I couldn't care less," said Shauntrece, but Penny had distracted her. Brian got his foot on the ball. He pushed it and started to get it clear of Shauntrece.

"The Daily Moos!" shouted Penny.

Brian stuck his tongue out of the side of his mouth and kicked the ball way downfield.

Mookie and some of the other kids clapped from the sidelines. Shauntrece looked angry.

"Lightning strikes!" said Brian with a grin. He felt terrific.

"Come on, Penny," shouted Coach Pereira. "We need that ball.

Penny ran to get the ball then trotted

to the sidelines with it.

"Where did you get that stupid Daily Moos joke?" Brian asked her.

"From Uncle Mike, of course," said Penny. She grinned at Brian. She handed the ball to Coach Pereira. Then she noticed that there were a bunch of kneepads lying on the wet grass. She ran to pick them up.

Penny heard Heather and Paul, a fourth-grader, talking. "Yeah, I know, he's a nerd," said Paul. "But I heard that his family has hired somebody to give him special lessons. He's keeping it a secret so it looks like he's getting better all on his own."

Penny wondered who they were talking about. There weren't many kids on the team who might be considered nerds except Brian.

"Yeah, somebody told me Lightning

Casanova's family will do anything to get him on the team."

Penny felt confused. She knew that Brian wasn't getting any special lessons. Or was he? Was Brian keeping something secret, even from her?

5

A Job for a Pea Brain Detective

"Tell me about your mystery coach," demanded Penny as they were walking home from practice.

"Huh?" asked Brian. "What are you talking about?"

"I heard some kids talking. They said our family is paying someone to give you special lessons. It makes me mad."

"Pea Brain, you've got rocks in your head," said Brian, He was still riding high from Coach Pereira's praise.

When Mrs. Casanova got home from

work, Penny went up to her. "It's not fair."

"What's not fair?" asked Mrs. Casanova.

"How come you're paying someone to teach Brian soccer. I'm gonna be a soccer player too, and I should get lessons too. Brian gets all the good stuff," said Penny. "And I don't get anything."

"We're not paying for special lessons for Brian," said Mrs. Casanova. "Except for violin lessons. But you said you didn't want to play the violin."

"I don't. I'm gonna play something cool like the drums."

"Not in this house," said Mrs. Casanova. "It's the violin or the piano, no drums."

Penny put her hands on her hips. "This has nothing to do with music."

"I promise you, Penny," said Mrs.

Casanova. "Brian is not getting anything special that you're not getting."

"Then why are people talking about it as if he is," asked Penny.

"Who's talking?" asked Mrs. Casanova.

"Never mind," said Penny. "I'll figure it out for myself."

For the next couple of days, Penny watched Brian's every move. Except for when she was in school, she didn't let him out of her sight. And it wasn't easy because the weather had turned really lousy with lots of drizzly rain. Penny got soaked watching Brian practice his soccer kicks by himself in the backyard.

There was no secret coach, nobody. Most of the time, Brian practiced by himself. He practiced the moves that Coach Pereira taught him and he tried to teach himself new moves out of the book from Uncle Mike.

Finally, one night as they were going to bed, Brian knocked on Penny's door and went in.

The drizzly day had turned into a real thunderstorm. The rain pelted against the windows. Penny hated thunderstorms. So did their cat, Flea. Flea was called Flea not because she had fleas, but because Mrs. Casanova had found her at a church flea market.

A blaze of lightning lit up the sky outside Penny's window. A few seconds later there was a loud crack of thunder. Penny gripped Flea's fur. Flea yelped. "Flea's scared of thunder," said Penny.

Brian didn't call Penny a scaredy-cat. "If you count the seconds between lightning and thunder, you can figure out how far away the storm is," he said. "I used to do that when I got scared."

"You got scared in thunderstorms too?"

"A little," admitted Brian. "It must run in the family.

A sharp flash of lightning lit up the sky. Penny closed her eyes and started counting, "One one thousand, two one thousand. . . "

Brian counted with her. At five one thousand, there was another loud roar of thunder. This time the thunder sounded like a monster truck crashing into Godzilla. Yet Penny didn't look quite as scared. "The storm is one mile away." said Brian. "Five seconds equals one mile."

Penny nodded. She played nervously with the collar of her rain forest T-shirt. Brian stroked Flea. "Okay, Penny, what's up? Why are you acting like my shadow? You've been following me around for days."

"I've been trying to find out about your secret coach," admitted Penny.

"I don't have a secret coach. Cross my heart and hope to die." Brian drew an X across his chest. Penny squinted. She knew her brother. He wouldn't cross his heart and hope to die unless he was telling the truth.

"Then why are the kids saying things about you?" asked Penny. "I heard them talking about it again. Everybody thinks that our family is paying a secret coach to give you lessons."

Brian groaned. "I can't believe it. It's so weird. I've found a sport I like and am good at, and whammo! Somebody's telling lies about me."

Penny's eyes opened wide. "I can help you," she said quietly.

"What can you do? Brian asked.

"I don't know," said Penny. "But I can listen. Nobody on the team pays any attention to me. They're all used to me being around."

"You could tell me if you hear any other rumors," admitted Brian. It was hard to believe that he was actually asking Penny for her help.

Penny looked up at Brian with her big eyes. "Ain't nobody going to spread lies about my brother." She jumped out of bed.

"Don't say ain't," corrected Brian.

Penny didn't pay him any attention. "I'm going to be the detective that saves the team!" she said, jumping up and down and startling Flea, who dug her claws into Brian's thigh.

"Penny, shh," warned Brian.

"Okay," said Penny, quieting down. "This is a job for a Pea Brain detective."

Brian had to smile. Penny usually hated being called Pea Brain, but here she was, actually using the name herself

It was on the tip of Brian's tongue to say something mean—that a Pea Brain couldn't solve a mystery. He held his tongue.

6

You Hurt Me, Man

Brian sat cross-legged on the ground, studying his book *All About Soccer*.

"What're you doing?" Penny asked. She was bored.

"I'm trying to learn how to do a banana kick," said Brian.

"I'd rather eat a banana," said Penny.

Brian read aloud from the book. "'The banana kick is one of the most difficult to master. It swerves and confuses the opposing team.'"

The pages of the book flew up in

Brian's face. "Penny, sit on this book while I try it."

Penny held down the pages of the book. "'To swerve the ball from left to right,'" Brian read, "'the kicker must make contact with the right side of the ball, using part of his instep.'"

"Or her instep," corrected Penny. "After all, when I'm seven, and I'm going to be a great soccer player too."

"Right," said Brian. He actually smiled. He walked backward almost fifty feet and then ran full tilt toward the ball. He tried to wrap the front part of his foot around the ball, but he overstepped and tripped, falling flat on his face.

It took him a minute to get up. Penny ran to him. "I'm okay," said Brian. He brushed himself off.

Penny squinched her eyes up. "Maybe if you just kick it from a few steps away,"

45

she said. "Don't take a running start."

"Why?" asked Brian.

"Because I heard Coach Pereira say there's more to soccer than just hitting the ball hard," said Penny. "Maybe you're working on the wrong thing."

Brian bit his lip. He *had* been concentrating on just hitting the ball hard. He hadn't realized that there were things he could do to control it.

Brian backed up just a few feet. He moved toward the ball, twisting his foot. The ball sailed in an arc, flying in an impressive curve.

"All right!" shouted Brian. "Now, that's a banana kick." Just then Mookie and some of the other kids from the team came up.

Brian waved to him. "I just did my first banana kick. Penny helped me figure it out."

"What did the boy banana say to the girl banana?" asked Penny.

"I don't know, Pea Brain," said Brian, but he said it as if he liked her.

"You've got a lot of appeal," Penny giggled. "It's a joke from Uncle Mike."

"Pretty funny," said Brian. "Get it, Mook the Nuke? You've got a lot of a peel like a banana peel."

"I get it," said Mookie. "Did lightning strike your house last night? You and Penny are acting weird. You're actually being human to each other."

"Well, sometimes we're a team," said Brian. "I can't wait to show Coach Pereira what I learned.

"Never mind that," said Mookie. "I am really mad at you."

Brian stared at his friend. "Why, because I practiced a banana kick without you? It's not that hard. I can teach you."

"Forget about that," said Mookie.

"This is much more important. You hurt my feelings. You hurt me, man."

"Mookie, what?" asked Brian. He couldn't think what he could have done to his friend.

"I didn't know that you were adopted too," said Mookie. "I'm your best friend. You've always known that I'm adopted, and that it's nothing to be ashamed of, but you kept it a secret from me."

Brian's mouth dropped open. "But I'm not adopted," he said.

"Yes, you are. You're the grandson of Pelé, the greatest soccer player of all time. That guy from Brazil. I never knew you spoke Spanish."

"They speak Portuguese in Brazil," said Penny.

"How did you know that, Pea Brain?" asked Brian.

"We study the rain forest in kindergarten, Brian Brain. That's why I sleep

in a rain forest T-shirt made of pure cotton."

"I thought you two weren't fighting anymore," said Mookie.

"Old habits die hard," muttered Brian. "But where did you hear that I was adopted?"

"It made me mad," said Mookie. "I can't believe you wouldn't tell me.

"I am *not* adopted."

"And they said that you're not really seven years old," added Mookie. "You're a little short for your age, but you're actually nine or ten."

"I am not," said Brian, "and you know it. How could I be from Brazil? My great-grandparents were from Genoa in Italy. Italy's got nothing to do with Brazil."

Brian narrowed his eyes. "Did you hear another rumor—that I've got some secret coach helping me."

Mookie wouldn't look at Brian. "Well, I heard something like that. I didn't believe that one. But the one about you being adopted really hurt."

"I told you. I'm not adopted. I can't be. I'm the spitting image of my Uncle Mike, my mom's brother. We've got the same red hair and freckles and ears. Believe me, I'd tell you the truth if I were adopted."

"Sometimes I wish he was adopted, then we wouldn't be related," said Penny.

"I'd still be your brother, Pea Brain."

"Oh, yeah," said Penny. "I guess you would, wouldn't you? No matter what." Penny took a step forward. "This rumor is another case for the Pea Brain detective. Brian, write down some notes for me."

"Why should I be your secretary?" asked Brian.

"Because in this case, I am the detective. And besides, I can only write my name."

Brian got a pad of paper. "There're so many kids on the soccer team," said Brian. "We'll never sort them out."

"Leave it to Pea Brain," said Penny importantly. "Okay, Mook the Nuke, who told you Brian was adopted?"

Mookie wiggled his nose. "I heard it first from Shauntrece. But she told me that she heard it from Natalia. But then I also heard it from Paul, and Paul said he heard it from Oscar."

"Wait," shouted Brian. "You're going too fast."

Penny started walking in circles. She stuck a finger in the air. "Well, Zap, you know, Natalia, might not have wanted you on the team," said Penny. "She thinks she's the best player. Maybe she's jealous. Write that down for motive."

"And Shauntrece, aka Flash, is the only other new kid on the team. She could be jealous too," added Mookie.

"What does aka stand for?" asked Penny. "Is it like okay?"

Brian snickered, but the truth was he was glad Penny had asked. He didn't know what it meant either.

"It means also known as," said Mookie. "I read it in a book." Mookie loved to read mystery books.

"Maybe Coach Pereira started the rumors," said Penny. "She's from Brazil, and those rumors were that somehow you were from Brazil. Maybe she's the one."

"What reason would Coach Pereira have for spreading rude rumors about me?" asked Brian.

Penny furrowed her brow. "Maybe she wants the other teams to hear them and think that you're such a hotshot that they don't have a chance. After all, your first big game is next week."

Brian shook his head. "This whole thing is turning my brain to mush."

"That's why you need a Pea Brain," said Penny cheerfully.

7

A Team
Is a Family

Coach Pereira gathered the team around her. "As you know our first game is next Saturday. Although we've had good practices, now is the time to prove that we are a team. The only way you can be a team is to trust one another."

Brian looked around suspiciously at his teammates. How could he trust them when one of them was spreading stories about him? He tried to take a deep breath. He hadn't had an asthma attack since he had begun soccer, but he could feel one coming on now.

He got out his inhaler from his knap-sack and squeezed it twice. He breathed in and felt his lungs clearing.

He looked around. Was it his imagina-tion, or was everyone staring at him, even Coach Pereira?

Coach Pereira coughed. "Before I make the final decisions for our starting lineup on Saturday, I'd like to have a full drill."

Brian put his inhaler back in his knap-sack. "Brian, you'll be a defender again,

one of our sweepers, but remember, in soccer, a defender also has to be an attacker."

Brian went out on the field. Natalia was on the attacking line, right next to Shauntrece. Oscar was the other sweeper. Oscar and Brian would have to play together.

Natalia attacked and got the ball into Brian and Oscar's territory.

Oscar kicked it out, trying to pass it to Brian, but the ball went too far. Brian galloped after it, but Shauntrece trapped it with her knee. She moved her head to the left. Brian fell for the fake, and Shauntrece triumphantly dribbled the ball right by him.

Brian went after her, furious as a bull. He tried to force Shauntrece to give up the ball.

"Go, Brian!" yelled Penny. But

Shauntrece was too fast for him.

She got ahead of him again. Brian took a big breath and headed after her.

He got to the ball a split second before Shauntrece. He planted himself and kicked the ball solidly out into midfield. It curved in the air, completely fooling Shauntrece and Natalia.

"What a banana kick! Great save, Brian!" shouted Coach Pereira. She blew her whistle. Brian trotted to the sidelines, grinning. He gave Oscar a thumbs-up sign. They had kept the attackers out of their territory.

Oscar ignored him. He and Shauntrece were whispering to each other. Brian watched them, tears coming to his eyes. Except for Mookie, he felt like he didn't have any friends on the team. He had found a sport that he loved, but there was nobody to share the good feelings with.

Coach Pereira signaled for Penny to bring everybody towels. Suddenly, Penny wrapped a towel around Natalia's neck! "You take that back!" screamed Penny at the top of her lungs.

In one swoop Coach Pereira picked up Penny around the middle of her waist and deposited her on the ground. "What's going on!" Coach Pereira demanded.

"Natalia said that Brian takes drugs to make him stronger!" yelled Penny.

"What!" roared Brian.

"Well, he's always breathing into that thing. It's just something I heard," said Natalia, brushing herself off. "Boy, you are one really strong little girl!" She looked admiringly at Penny.

Coach Pereira was furious. "Everyone listen up. A house divided cannot stand. You are either on this team or you are

not." She looked around at everyone angrily. "I know from Brian's application that he has asthma. Brian's doctor gives him asthma medication, but that is not the point. The point is that either this group pulls together as a family and as a team or we will lose every game. Even if we don't lose it won't matter. Every great team behaves as a family. Problems have to be worked out within our circle. And the circle has to include everyone. Does everybody understand what I mean?"

Each kid on the team nodded, but none of them would look the others in the eye. Their heads hung low. Penny caught Brian's eye. She knew what Brian was thinking. This group was not a family. They were not a team.

The Wheels
of Justice

"I've got a plan," said Penny the next day.

Brian looked at her. He couldn't ever remember feeling so down. Everything that Coach Pereira said about a team being a family rang true, but he just couldn't see how anything would change.

"What plan?" asked Brian.

"I figured out how to catch the person who's been spreading those rude rumors about you."

"Penny, I've got a big game coming up

on Saturday. I have enough to worry
about."

"Leave it to me," said Penny. "By
tonight, this will all be settled."

Penny went to Mookie. She told him
that she knew he wasn't starting the
rumors. "You wouldn't have been so up-
set about hearing that Brian was adopted
if it had been you. Besides I need an ally
on the team, and I've got to trust you."

Penny told Mookie her plan.

He grinned. "You know, you've got an evil mind," he said.

"Thank you," said Penny. She knew a compliment when she heard one.

At practice, Penny went to the group that had been spreading the rumors about Brian. First she talked to Shauntrece. Penny asked her if she could keep a secret.

"Of course, I can," said Shauntrece. Penny tried not to make a face. The only way her plan would work was if somebody could *not* keep a secret.

"Brian and I have an uncle. His first name is Mike, but everyone calls him Big Beef. He's a famous football player. That's why Brian's such a great athlete. Uncle Big Beef is coming to dinner tonight so that he can give Brian some pointers. That's not a rumor. That's the truth. But please don't tell anyone because Big Beef hates it when people bother him and ask for his autograph."

Then Penny went to Oscar and asked him if he could keep a secret. She told Oscar that her Uncle Michael was coming to town. "He's the greatest basketball player in Italy," she said. "And you know Italy has some of the best basketball players in the world."

Next Penny went to Natalia and told her that her Aunt Sarah was coming. "Aunt Sarah was an Olympic ice skater," bragged Penny. "She won the gold medal. That's where Lightning gets his fast moves."

"Lightning?" repeated Natalia.

"You know, Brian . . . my brother!"

After Penny finished her rounds of the team, she came back from the sidelines, looking elated.

"What are you doing?" Brian asked.

"I'm setting the wheels of justice in motion," said Penny.

"What are the wheels of justice?" Brian asked.

"It's something I heard on TV," said Penny. "It means that the bad guy gets what he deserves. It means that the girl or boy who messes with my brother is going to be very sorry."

In or Out

Later the next day, Uncle Mike and Aunt Sarah arrived from the airport. Uncle Mike loved bacon cheeseburgers, but nobody had ever called him Big Beef. Also nobody had ever confused Uncle Mike for a basketball player. He was only five foot six, pudgy and bald.

Aunt Sarah had never been an Olympic ice skater. The only way she liked ice was in a big glass of iced tea.

"Guess what, Uncle Mike," said Penny. "Brian doesn't take after you after

69

all. He's good at soccer."

"Penny," warned her mother, starting to blush.

Uncle Mike laughed. He might not be tall or full of muscles or have a lot of hair, but he had a great laugh.

"That's okay, Penny," he said. He winked at his nephew. "I bet your mom said she was worried that you were just like me. I was a terminal klutz at sports. That's why I sent you my friend's book."

"It helped, Uncle Mike," said Brian.

"And you, Penny, I have a special book for you too. I wanted to give it to you in person."

Penny ripped off the wrapping paper. She loved presents.

She whooped when she saw the funny pictures on the cover. Uncle Mike read her the title, "*The World's Worst Riddles.*"

"In this case, 'worst' is a compliment,"

said Uncle Mike. "I marked some that you might want to use right away." Penny flipped the pages.

Uncle Mike pointed to one and whispered in Penny's ear. "Why was Cinderella thrown off the soccer team?" Penny repeated.

Brian shook his head. "I don't know."

"Because she kept running away from the ball," said Penny. She shrieked.

Mr. and Mrs. Casanova groaned. It was considered polite to groan at Uncle Mike's jokes.

"Come on, kids," said Mr. Casanova. "Help me bring out the food. The fire should be ready. Uncle Mike, in honor or your arrival, we're going to have a big barbecue. Naturally, we've made enough for an army. Hot dogs, hamburgers, spareribs, the works. I'm the cook."

"Knock, knock," said Uncle Mike.

"Who's there?" asked Penny.

"Cook."

"Cook who?" asked Penny.

"Cuckoo yourself. I didn't come here to be insulted." said Uncle Mike. He took Penny's hand.

They all went into the backyard. It wasn't long before the smell of the spareribs cooking made everybody's mouths water.

Penny looked at her watch. If her plot to catch the person who was spreading the rumors was working, Mookie should have been there by now with one of the other kids from the team.

Penny looked up. Suddenly Shauntrece was in the backyard with Paul.

"Ah ha!" said Penny. "You must be wanting to meet my uncle Big Beef."

"Yeah," said Paul. Shauntrece said he was a great football player. Where's your uncle."

Uncle Mike waved a sparerib.

"He doesn't look like a football player," said Paul.

Just then Natalia showed up with her cousin Jasmine and a couple of other kids from the team. "My cousin Jasmine is an ice skater," said Natalia. "She wanted to meet your Aunt Sarah."

Penny's mother and Aunt Sarah stared at each other. "Ice skater?" repeated Aunt Sarah. She giggled.

"Penny, what's going on?" Brian asked.

Penny didn't answer. The next moment, Mookie showed up in the backyard with Oscar. Soon the backyard was filled with kids from the team.

Mookie looked very embarrassed when he saw the other kids. "Penny," groaned Mookie. "It didn't work. Everybody told everybody!"

"I think I goofed," said Penny.

"What did you do?" asked Brian. He was sounding a little panicked. All the kids from the team who had shown up gathered in a huddle. They looked up and glared at Penny.

"Hey, Casanova," shouted Shauntrece. "We want to talk to you."

"One minute," yelled Brian.

"Not you, Casanova. Your sister. She's the one who lied to all of us."

"Don't call my sister a liar," said Brian.

Penny tugged at Brian's sleeve. "I did lie a little. But I did it because I was being a detective. I told everybody a different story about Uncle Mike and Aunt Sarah. I figured the one who told the rumor to Mookie would be the one who was spreading rumors about you. But it didn't work."

"Don't get mad at her," said Mookie.

He looked around at all his teammates. "I thought it would work too. But I forgot that *everybody* on this team spreads rumors."

Penny put her hands on her hips. "I just wanted to catch the rude rowdy person who started the lies, Brian."

Oscar was staring at Uncle Mike. "You're not a basketball player, are you?"

Uncle Mike shook his head. "Do you know the poet of basketball?"

"Who?" asked Oscar

"Longfellow," said Uncle Mike.

"That's not very funny," muttered Oscar.

"Oscar," shouted Shauntrece. "Enough with the jokes. Come over here. It's time we figured out who's been starting these rumors. They're tearing our team apart."

"Thanks," said Brian. "Ever since I started playing soccer, Penny and I keep hearing weird stories about me."

"I can remember the first one," piped up Penny. "You all thought that our family was paying for a special coach for Brian."

"I heard that one from you, Natalia," said Paul. "You called me on the phone and told me."

"I heard it from Shauntrece," said Natalia. "I remember the phone call."

"I heard it from Oscar," said Shauntrece.

Oscar wouldn't look at his teammates. "Well, I heard it from this pip-squeak." He pointed to Penny.

"Me!" squawked Penny. "I wouldn't tell a lie about my brother."

"I heard you say he was getting secrets from his uncle Mike." said Oscar.

Penny hit her forehead with her palm. She gave Brian a guilty look. "Well, you did get that book from Uncle Mike. I might have said you were learning secrets. But I didn't say you had a secret coach."

"That's how rumors change," said Brian. "But what about the other ones. The one that I was the adopted grandson of Pelé. And the one that I took drugs. Those weren't just rude, they were nasty. And I know Penny didn't start them."

"I heard the one about your being adopted from Natalia," said Shauntrece.

"I heard it from Paul and Shauntrece," said Mookie.

"I heard it from Oscar," said Natalia.

"I heard it from Oscar too," said Paul.

Everybody looked at Oscar.

It was the same for the one about Brian's asthma drugs.

Penny glanced up. She realized that her parents and Uncle Mike and Aunt

Sarah were staring at them.

Penny bit her lip. She liked being the detective. She didn't want the adults getting involved.

"I think we should all talk to Oscar in Brian's room," said Penny.

"My room!" shrieked Brian.

"My room's too small. And we need to deal with him in private," said Penny.

Brian led the whole gang into his room. It was extremely neat and now it was extremely crowded.

Brian took a menacing step toward Oscar. "Why? Why have you been spreading those rumors about me?"

"I don't have to stick around for this," said Oscar.

Brian grabbed his arm. Oscar stared down at the rug. "Why?" Brian demanded.

The other kids circled Oscar. Oscar

lost his look of nastiness. He looked scared. "I was always the star defender," said Oscar. "Coach Pereira started telling everybody how good you were. I wanted to make you look bad."

Brian shook his head. "Oscar, we're teammates."

"Huh," said Penny. "Aren't you gonna punch out his clock? Aren't you gonna march him to Coach Pereira and turn him in for spreading rude rumors?"

"It wouldn't make us a team," said Brian. He looked at Shauntrece and the other kids. "Remember what Coach Pereira said. We're either a team or we're not. We're in the circle or we're not. Oscar tried to keep me out of the circle. If I tried to keep him out, we'd be right back where we started. We all need each other."

"Brian's right," said Shauntrece. "The

man is making sense."

"Thanks," said Brian.

"He's not a man. He's still a kid," said Penny.

Oscar wouldn't look at Brian or at any of the other kids. He was making Brian mad. "Look at me," Brian insisted. He shook Oscar's arm. "Are you in or are you out!"

"Before you came, Coach Pereira said I was the best young defender she had ever seen."

"In or out?" repeated Brian.

Oscar raised his eyes. He looked at his teammates. "In," he said.

Everyone cheered and patted one another on the back.

Penny couldn't believe it. "Wait! I solved the mystery, and he doesn't get punished?"

"Penny, you didn't exactly solve it,"

said Brian. "But you got the ball rolling. And Oscar is never going to start another rumor again. Right, Oscar?"

"Right," said Oscar.

"But what's his punishment!" insisted Penny.

"It's not the punishment that counts," said Brian. "It's the team."

10

The Pea Brain for It

Brian jumped up and down on the edge of the soccer field, trying to stay relaxed. His parents had come to watch the game along with Aunt Sarah and Uncle Mike. Everybody was expecting him to be terrific. Penny was busy getting towels and kneepads to everyone who needed them.

Brian watched the other team finish their warm-ups. They looked good.

Coach Pereira blew her whistle. "All right, kids. This is our first big test. How many people are feeling a little bit scared and nervous right now?"

At first nobody raised his or her hand. Brian and Oscar looked at each other. Then they both raised their hands together.

Coach Pereira nodded at them. "Oscar and Brian, it takes a brave player to admit being scared. Competition brings out the very best and the very worst in us. But if you stick with it, it's going to bring out the best. And the fear will go away. The more you try to do your best, the less scared you will be."

Oscar raised his hand again. "Coach Pereira, I've got to say something to the team. When Brian first joined us, I started telling you kids some things about him. They weren't true. I was scared that he was going to take my place."

The rest of the team was silent. Coach Pereira looked down at her playbook. "Brian and Oscar," she said. "You're both playing in the backfield today. Brian, you'll be the left sweeper. Oscar you'll be the right. I want the two of you to defend our territory like eagles."

Brian and Oscar looked at each other. Then there was no longer time to think. The team had to take the field.

At the whistle, Shauntrece, who was playing center, tried to drive the ball too fast and lost control of it. The other team's defender swooped down on the ball and kicked it sharply out to their line.

Oscar and Brian looked at each other. They knew the ball was coming down fast toward their goalie. They had to defend their territory.

Brian moved up to tackle the wing. The wing tried to evade him, but Brian stuck with her like glue.

He got the ball away from her and passed the ball to Oscar so that Oscar

could shoot it out.

"Lightning! Lightning!" shouted Penny from the sidelines. She waved her hands in the air and got everyone in the stands to join her in the cheer.

"Lightning! Lightning!" shouted Uncle Mike at the top of his lungs. He had a very loud voice.

The referee blew his whistle and stopped the game.

Coach Pereira was furious. "Why did you stop the game!" she shouted, running out onto the field. "My team had the momentum."

The referee looked up at the bright blue sky and scratched his head. "Lightning!" he said. "I can't let the game go on if there's lightning around."

Coach Pereira rolled her eyes. She explained that "Lightning" was the nickname for Brian Casanova, one of her players. Coach Pereira smiled. "One of my best players," she added.

The referee looked embarrassed. He blew his whistle for the game to continue.

Shauntrece got the ball again, and this time she and Natalia weaved their way downfield and Natalia got a goal.

That one goal was all they needed. Brian and Oscar didn't let the other team score once. The final score was 1–0.

Afterward, Oscar and Brian hugged each other and exchanged high fives.

Then Penny ran up to Brian. "We won!" he said.

Penny grinned. "You were great."

Brian was beaming. "In two years, you'll be a great soccer player, too," he said.

"Do you think so?" asked Penny.

Brian nodded. He rapped his knuckles on the top of Penny's head, but not too hard, almost gently. "Yeah," he said. "You've already got the pea brain for it."